This edition published by Parragon Books Ltd in 2016

Parragon Books Ltd
Chartist House
15–17 Trim Street
Bath BA1 1HA, UK
www.parragon.com

ISBN 978-1-4748-5412-2

Printed in China

THE
ORIGIN STORIES

Bath • New York • Cologne • Melbourne • Delhi
Hong Kong • Shenzhen • Singapore

Have you ever felt lonely? Sad? Powerless? Peter Parker felt that way every day. He was a student at Midtown High. Peter enjoyed his classes and studied hard, but he didn't have many friends. The other kids at school made fun of him for being a good student. It made Peter feel very small.

But nothing could stop Peter from enjoying science. He was the best student Midtown High had seen in many years, and his teachers were sure that he would grow up to be a famous scientist. He loved experimenting in the lab and coming up with new inventions.

Peter's family were very proud of him. He lived with his Aunt May and Uncle Ben in Queens, New York. Peter loved them more than anything, and whenever he felt sad in school, he just reminded himself that he'd soon be home, and he'd start to smile.

Even though the other kids at school didn't like him, Peter never stopped trying to be friendly. He had heard that there would be a great demonstration in the Science Hall, so he asked some of the other kids if they wanted to join him.

They just laughed at Peter. One of the kids, a bully named Flash Thompson, pushed him to the ground, making him drop all his school books.

Angry and upset, Peter gathered up his books and
went to the demonstration alone.

By the time Peter arrived at the Science Hall, he had forgotten all about Flash Thompson and the other kids. All he could think about was the experiment. The scientists were going to try to control a radioactive wave. It was so exciting! Peter eagerly looked on ...

... but so did something else.

Finally, the rays were ready.
The audience gathered round.
The demonstration was about
to begin!

Peter stared in awe as the rays were activated. He was thrilled to be there, in the company of such brilliant scientists. He wanted to be just like them one day – smart, talented ... amazing!

Everyone was so fascinated, no one noticed the tiny spider that descended between the rays just as they were activated....

The rays hit the spider, turning it radioactive. The spider fell towards the ground, and as it died, it bit the nearest living thing ...

... which happened to be Peter Parker.

Peter suddenly felt weak and tired. The room began to spin. The scientists noticed that he looked ill and offered to help him. But Peter just wanted to get out of the dark laboratory and into the fresh air. He staggered outside, barely able to see where he was going....

Peter felt a sudden, peculiar tingling in his head. It was a strange, nagging, urging feeling that he had never felt before. It seemed to be saying that he was in danger. The only thing he knew for sure was that he was meant to react somehow ...

... to do something.

So he did.

Peter was sure he must be dreaming.
He couldn't really be climbing a wall.
It wasn't possible. But somehow he
kept putting one hand above the other,
climbing higher and higher....

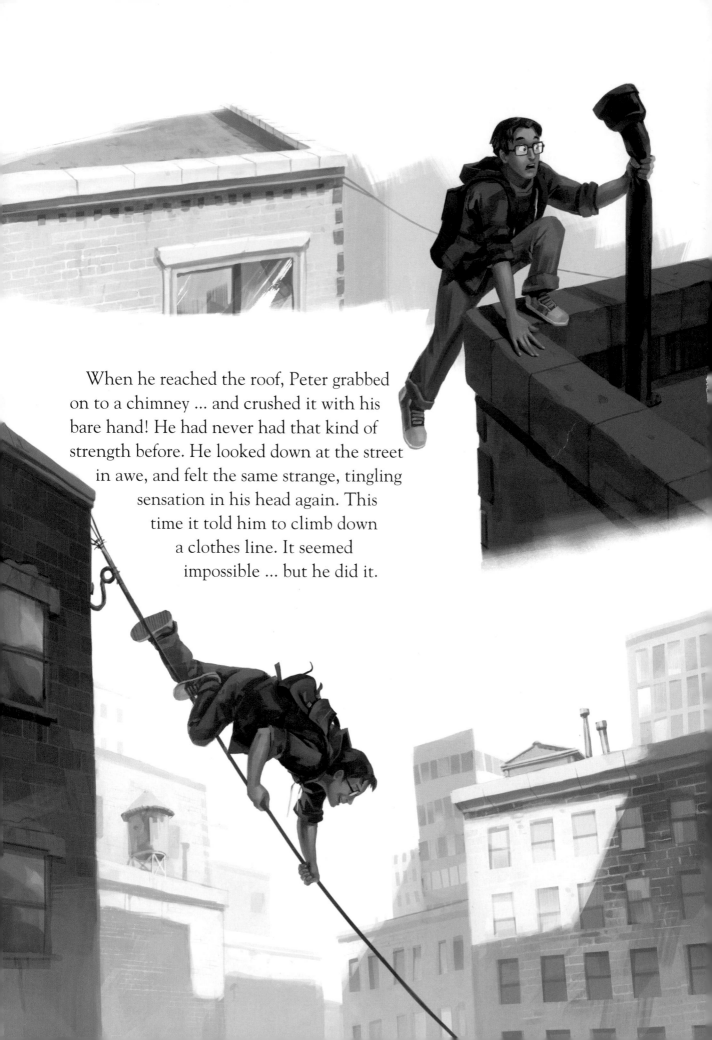

When he reached the roof, Peter grabbed
on to a chimney ... and crushed it with his
bare hand! He had never had that kind of
strength before. He looked down at the street
in awe, and felt the same strange, tingling
sensation in his head again. This
time it told him to climb down
a clothes line. It seemed
impossible ... but he did it.

Peter was amazed. How could this be happening to him? He remembered feeling strange right after he was bitten by the spider in the lab – and suddenly, he realized where his new abilities had come from. The spider must have been changed by the experiment. Then, when it bit Peter, it had given its powers to him!

As he wandered home, a sign outside an old wrestling theatre caught his eye. It would be the perfect way for him to test his new-found abilities.

Peter rushed home ...

... and then he rushed straight back out.
He wore a disguise so that no one could make fun of him if his plan failed. He'd been teased and taunted enough.

Peter was going to test his new powers on a brutish wrestler called Crusher Hogan.

When Peter challenged him, Crusher Hogan laughed. The wrestler soon found out that that was a big mistake!

Peter was paid well for the victory, and a man in the crowd even asked if he wanted to be on TV! Things seemed to be working out for him at last.

And things just kept getting better. Aunt May and Uncle Ben saved up to buy Peter a new, special microscope for his experiments. His uncle reminded Peter that science was knowledge, and knowledge was power.

"And with great power comes great responsibility," Uncle Ben told him.

Peter used his new microscope and his chemistry set to create a special fluid with the strength and stickiness of a spider's web.

He created devices that could spin the fluid into webs the same way a spider would. He called them his web-shooters. Then he designed a sleek new costume....

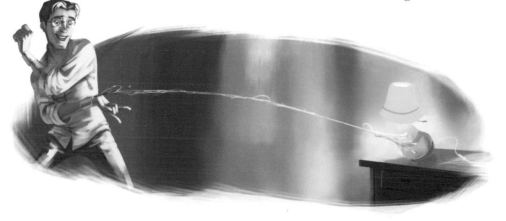

All he needed now was a stage name. Something that told the world who he was and what he could do. It could be nothing other than ... the Amazing Spider-Man!

Peter's TV appearances were a huge hit.
Everyone was amazed by the Spider-Man
as he climbed walls, spun webs and swung
from the ceiling.

Soon everyone wanted a piece of Spider-Man. Peter began to feel important, popular ... and powerful. No one would ever be able to push him around again, not with his amazing powers. Peter daydreamed about fame and celebrity. His new life began to change him.

One day, after another TV appearance, a security guard in the studio called for Peter's help. He was chasing a thief down the hall. But Peter ignored him and the thief escaped.

But Peter didn't care. He had great power. And from now on, he only needed to look out for one person – himself.

But one night on his way home from a TV performance, Peter arrived to find police cars parked outside his aunt and uncle's house.

Peter knew something was terribly wrong, and he was right.

His Uncle Ben
had been killed
by a criminal. The
police officers told
Peter not to worry. They
had cornered the crook at an
old waterfront warehouse.

Peter immediately ran upstairs,

put on his costume ...

... and swung across the city to catch the criminal and avenge his uncle.

At last, Peter arrived at the warehouse. He landed on the far wall. The thief was stunned.

And that's when Spider-Man sprung into action!

The man reached for his gun, but Peter was too fast....

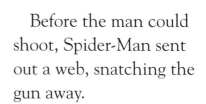

Before the man could shoot, Spider-Man sent out a web, snatching the gun away.

The crook's hat flew from his head, and Peter finally got a good look at him.

As he looked at the crook, something slowly dawned on him. Peter felt a heavy weight in his chest. It couldn't be. But it was. The man who had killed his uncle was the same man he allowed to escape into the elevator at the studio.

If only Peter had stopped him then! If only he had not acted so selfishly!

Stunned, Peter tied up the criminal in webbing and dangled him from a street lamp for the police to find. The most Peter could do now was prevent him from hurting anyone else. Through the haze of his grief, Peter realized something. He had not chosen these abilities, but it was his obligation to use them for good.

It was not about money or fame or any of the other rewards his power could give him. He had finally realized that what his Uncle Ben had told him was true: with great power comes great responsibility.

And that was the rule that Peter Parker lived by
from that day forward.

This is Iron Man. He's a one-man crime-fighting machine! His amazing armour was made using cutting-edge technology. He can fly and shoot powerful beams of energy from his hands, and he's invincible to enemy attack. He is the ultimate hero.

Villains such as Titanium Man and Iron Monger use this technology for their own evil purposes. They cause destruction and chaos.

That's when Iron Man steps in.

Iron Man has many enemies,
and he has many imitators ...

... but he has no equal.
No one is strong enough to defeat him.

But it wasn't always like this.
Iron Man's armour wasn't always this sleek, or this powerful.
He wasn't always able to defeat villains this easily.

In fact, when he first became Iron Man, his armour didn't even shine.

But if you really want to know how Iron Man was born, we need to start with the man behind the mask.

We need to start with Tony Stark.

Once, Tony was just a regular guy – but a very rich one. He had so much money that he could go anywhere. He liked to relax and have fun, and he enjoyed the finer things in life.

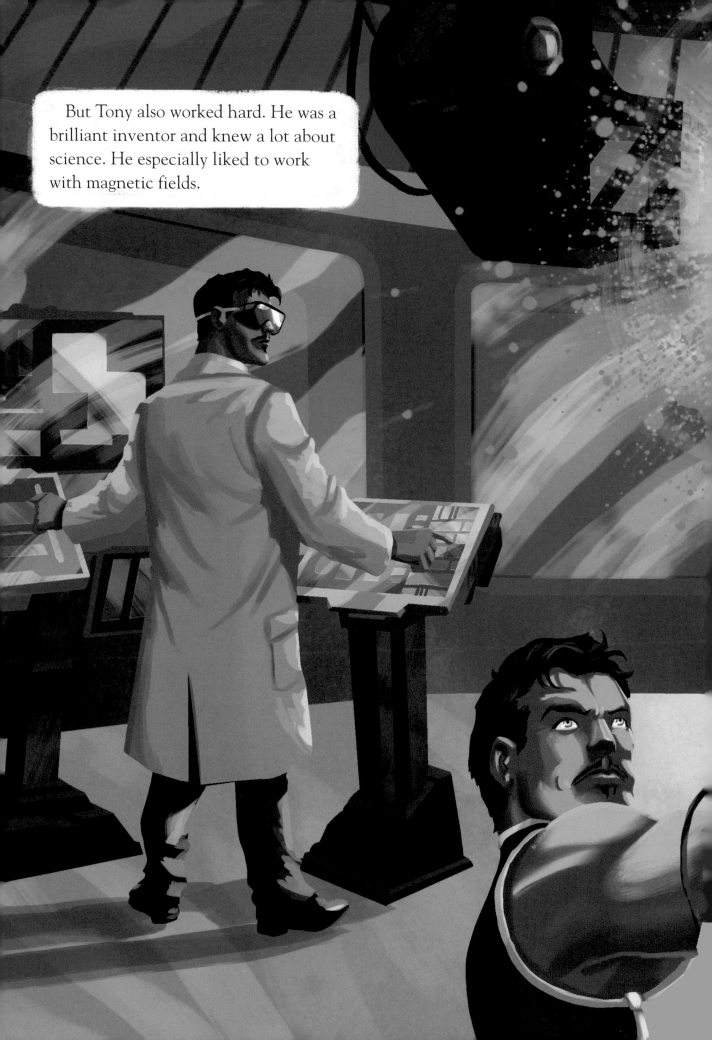

But Tony also worked hard. He was a brilliant inventor and knew a lot about science. He especially liked to work with magnetic fields.

Using them, he created a powerful new energy force that he called repulsor technology. The military was interested in Tony's work, and invited him to visit a secret Army lab.

It was there that Tony's life was changed forever.
An enemy army attacked, and there was a huge explosion.
Tony was seriously hurt.

Tony was very famous, and the enemy soldiers recognized him straight away. They knew all about his inventions. They took him prisoner and brought him back to their camp.

Then, they tossed Tony in a prison cell filled with electronic and mechanical equipment, and told him to get to work. They wanted him to create a mighty, new weapon for them.

But Tony felt sick and weak. And before the enemy soldiers left the tiny cell, they told Tony that his heart had been hurt in the blast. He did not have much longer to live.

Tony soon found he was not alone in the cell. The enemy had captured another famous scientist – Professor Yinsen. The enemy wanted the two men to work together on the great weapon.

But Professor Yinsen had other ideas –
he had thought of a way to keep Tony alive!

The two men worked tirelessly to create something that would save Tony's life, and at the same time, help them to escape the prison!

Finally, the men completed the device that Tony would always need to wear on his chest to keep his heart beating.

But that wasn't all they had created.

Using Tony's repulsors, they had built boots that could help a man fly!

Gloves that could crush st

And a helmet that could protect a man from the most terrible blast!

Tony put on the armour ...

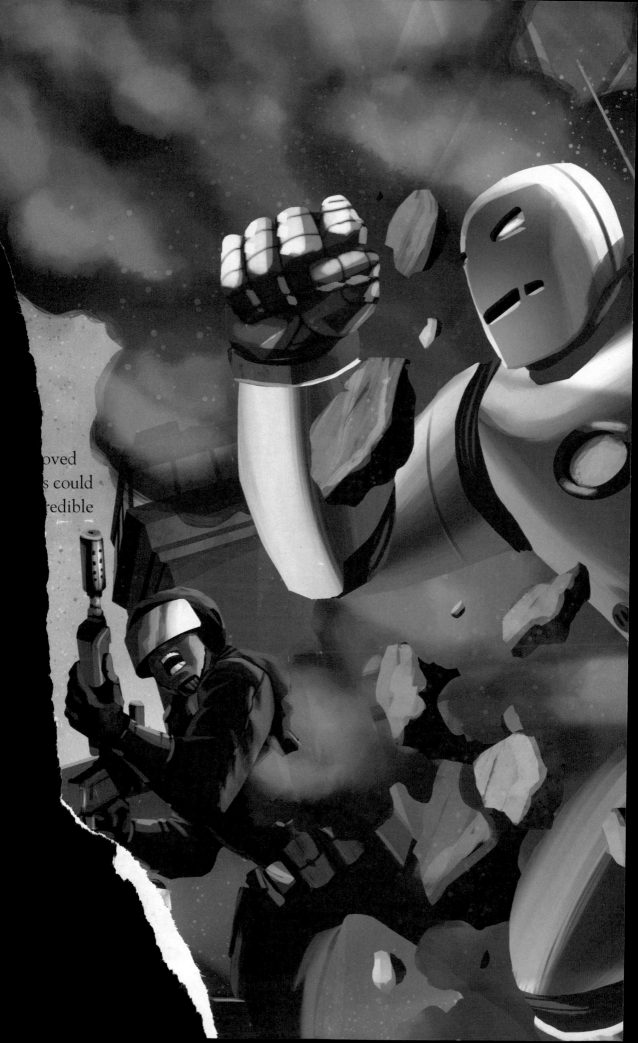

Having escaped from prison, Tony flew back home.

But almost as soon as he got there, he realized that he could now help where others couldn't.

Tony to the rescue! He was strong, unstoppable, frightening ... maybe a little too frightening.

Tony had an idea. He thought that Iron Man needed something as smooth and stylish as he was.

He needed to create a lighter suit.

All he needed was for his chest plate to remain attached. Everything else could be changed.

Tony perfected his armour.

And the indestructible Iron Man was born again!

And as Iron Man, Tony never stops fighting.

He protects people at home ...

... and around the world.

And when he's not fighting for justice as Iron Man, Tony runs his company, Stark Industries.

Stark Industries might need Tony to be a businessman, but with new villains attacking every day ...

... Tony is always
ready to put on his
mighty armour ...

... and become the invincible Iron Man!